Written by Aysha Ahmed
Illustrations by Bella & Sophia

Georgie

Bumblebee Books
London

A CIP catalogue record for this title is
available from the British Library.

ISBN: 978-1-83934-083-3

Bumblebee Books is an imprint of
Olympia Publishers.

First Published in 2021

Bumblebee Books
Tallis House
2 Tallis Street
London
EC4Y 0AB

Printed in Great Britain

www.olympiapublishers.com

Dedication

Zakariya, Amal, Mariyam, Aiesha Boshofa, Abbilo, Josef and Jonas

Georgie was a pirate who had sailed the seven seas,
With curly ginger hair and purple dungarees.

She sang to the dolphins and danced under the moon
At shimmery pearl parties in a mermaid's blue lagoon.

But what she loved best of all was reading a good book,
About magic and dragons or learning how to cook.

In all her favourite stories no one ventured all alone,
They had friends by their side and somewhere to call home.

Georgie closed her books and sighed, "I wish I had a friend.
We'd dress up as knights and fight! But only just pretend."

That night a stormy wind raged, it blew and blew and blew
Georgie and her ship to land! "Has my wish come true?!"

But the people of the town turned in shock and stared aghast!
They'd never seen a **PIRATE** with a ship and sail and mast.

The children screamed and clutched their mums, scared of what she'd want.
"You're not welcome here!" declared the mayor with a grunt.

"Ahoy there!" cried Georgie. "I'm tired of sailing all alone.
It's not fun to wrestle monster squids all on your own."

The children laughed, "Look at the holes and mud splattered on her dress!"
"She talks funny for a girl!" they sneered. "Her hair's a smelly mess!"

Georgie looked down and sniffed her dungarees and shoe.
"Sniff. That's not mud,"she said. "I'm sure it's just squid poo.
I can wash and comb these locks and these holes each tell a tale.
Once trapped in the belly of a one-eyed killer whale!"

Young and old gathered round listening in awe
To hear of sea monsters with a ferocious roar!
And coral caves of jewels and gold guarded by unicorns
Who once trapped greedy pirates with their pointy unihorns.

Then a girl came forward, "I'm **Flick**,"she said, "and this is my dog **Bear**.
We don't have very much but we'd be happier to share."

And summer through to spring they did everything together,
From mending boats to patching roofs in stormy weather.

Georgie helped **Flick** to read the stars up in the sky,
She taught Bear to whistle to call dolphins swimming by.
She made a hearty pirate stew of tatties, beef and kale,
And the children begged Georgie to tell tale after tale.

Alas the waves called out to her and Georgie longed to be at Sea,
But as she climbed on board her ship, Georgie felt uneasy.

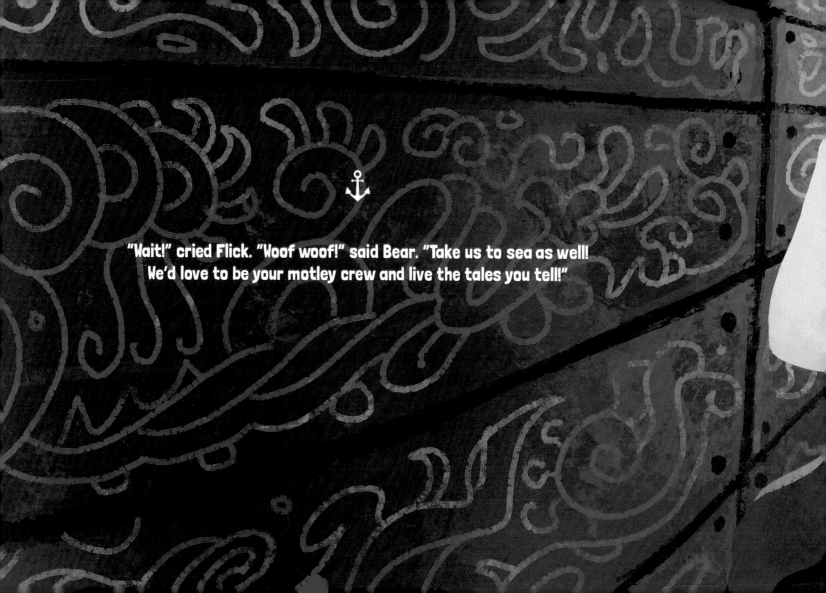

"Wait!" cried Flick. "Woof woof!" said Bear. "Take us to sea as well!
We'd love to be your motley crew and live the tales you tell!"

"Climb aboard mateys!" Georgie cried. "What a pleasure!
I've found my family and that is priceless treasure!

We're set for adventure but we won't be gone for long."
"Come back soon!" cried the mayor. "To the home where you belong."

About the Author and Illustrator

Aysha and Bella met at medical school almost twenty years ago and have been great friends ever since. They've found working together on this picture book a welcome break from their busy lives of balancing work and their small families. What started as a hobby led to surprisingly long hours but all in the hope that children will enjoy the story of *Georgie* just as much as they did in creating it!